Mini Sagas

Mini Marvels

WORCESTERSHIRE & THE WEST MIDLANDS

CW00733668

First published in Great Britain in 2010 by
Young Writers, Remus House, Coltsfoot Drive,
Peterborough, PE2 9JX
Tel (01733) 890066 Fax (01733) 313524
Website: www.youngwriters.co.uk

All Rights Reserved
© Copyright Contributors 2010
SB ISBN 978-1-84924-960-7

Disclaimer
Young Writers has maintained every effort
to publish stories that will not cause offence.
Any stories, events or activities relating to individuals
should be read as fictional pieces and not construed
as real-life character portrayal.

Foreword

Since Young Writers was established in 1990, our aim has been to promote and encourage written creativity amongst children and young adults. By giving aspiring young authors the chance to be published, Young Writers effectively nurtures the creative talents of the next generation, allowing their confidence and writing ability to grow.

With our latest fun competition, *The Adventure Starts Here ...* , secondary school children nationwide were given the tricky challenge of writing a story with a beginning, middle and an end in just fifty words.

The diverse and imaginative range of entries made the selection process a difficult but enjoyable task with stories chosen on the basis of style, expression, flair and technical skill. A fascinating glimpse into the imaginations of the future, we hope you will agree that this entertaining collection is one that will amuse and inspire the whole family.

Contents

Adcote School for Girls, Shrewsbury

Gabrielle Green (14) 1
Ophelia Gillyon (13) 2
Georgina Mary Kennedy Welsh (13) 3
Molly Victoria Jones (13) 4

Alcester High School, Alcester

Elle Irving (14) 5
Jessica Carter (14) 6
Esther Parr (13) 7
Ally Broomfield-Gull (12) 8
Laura Giles (13) 9
Joshua Brookes (12) 10
Adam Kenyon (12) 11
Timothy Bradley (13) 12
Laura Willcox (12) 13
Emily Sabin (12) 14
Jason Batts (12) 15
Josh Godson (12) 16
Ben Wiltshire (15) 17
James Reeves (14) 18
Marianne Hoy (15) 19

Luis Sone (15) 20
Andrew Ward (14) 21
Ellie Muitt (14) 22
Charlotte Tudberry (13) 23
Samuel Bevins (13) 24
Christian Rushton (14) 25
Chiara Ploteghen (14) 26
Isabel Smith (14) 27
Rebecca Mottram (13) 28
Jake Williams (14) 29
Emma Garrett (13) 30
Morgan Alcock (13) 31
Beth Radbourne (14) 32
Bryn Sanford (13) 33
Zak Gavin (14) 34
Molly Malin (13) 35
Nina Gunton (12) 36
Alexander Cox (13) 37
Hannah Clury (12) 38
Ben Godson (12) 39
Laura Smith (14) 40
Georgia Buxton (14) 41

Jack Baker (13) 42
Katherine Hudson (13) 43
Mollie-Anne Shepherd (13) 44
Caroline Stewart (13) 45
Nicole Clay-Noonan (13) 46
Bethan Leahy (12) 47
Leah Ballinger (13) 48
Natalie Price (14) 49
Max Tarrant (13) 50

Bristnall Hall Technology College, Oldbury

Jerome Bailey (13) 51
Callum Cleary (12) 52
Alex Sandhu (12) 53
Phoebe Hinton-Sheley (13) 54
Aiden Ashton (13) 55
Amber Marshall (12) 56
Ryan Colledge (13) 57
Rowena Ellis (12) 58
Jessica Clews (12) 59
Emily Parsons (12) 60
Katie McCarron (12) 61
Matthew Gibson (12) 62
Heather Frear (12) 63
Katie Nikolic (13) 64

Jonathan Davies (12) 65
Beth Henderson (12) 66
Harriet Hynes (12) 67
Clare Gardner (12) 68
Aneesa Malik (13) 69
Dalton Cooper (12) 70
Taylor Bromley (12) 71
Melissa Limbrick (13) 72
Alex Smith (12) 73
Jodie Davis (12) 74
Elise Caddick (12) 75
Dionne Bailey (12) 76
Dominika Pietrak (12) 77

Bromsgrove School, Bromsgrove

Brett Huxley (14) 78
Laura-May Matthews (15) 79
James Lay (15) 80
James Hey (15) 81
Sophie Haycock-Jones (14) 82
Thomas Gretton (14) 83
Sam Coope (14) 84
Rachel Clare (14) 85
Emma Rowell (13) 86
Sam Adamson (13) 87
George Goucher (13) 88

Sam Rose (13)..89
Stephanie Swatkins (13) 90
Bethan Luckman (13) 91
Carliene Silk (13) 92
Alexander Berwick (13)..............................93
Amy Foster (13) 94
Asher Hardy (14).......................................95
Abbie-May Griffiths (14) 96
Matthew Budge (13)..................................97
Andrea Ellins (13) 98
Montana Bent (14).....................................99
George Toft 100
Edward Philp (15)....................................101
Ivan Taptygin (14) 102
Calum Cooper (14) 103

Dodderhill School, Droitwich Spa

Emmeline Charlotte Trenchard-Mole (12) 104
Olivia Cox (11)...105
Alexandra Stephenson (11) 106
Katie Edgington (12).................................107
Phoebe Clayton (12) 108
Isobel Fox (12)...109
Shannon Holly Stowe (11)........................110
Micayla Fradd (11)....................................111
Felicity Smith-Maxwell (11).......................112

Emma Bridges (11)...................................113
Hannah Jones (11) 114
Emily Meredith (11)..................................115
Alice Fish (11)..116
Eleanor Kinsman (12)...............................117
Isabelle Palmer (12).................................118
Georgina Reece (11).................................119
Molly Everitt (13).....................................120
Matilda Hallett (13)..................................121
Paige Conlon (13).....................................122
Rebecca Hardy (13)..................................123
Lydia Tainty (13) 124
Abigail Smith (13) 125
Emily Webster (14)...................................126
Amelia Clancy (13)...................................127
Heidi Fellows (14).....................................128
Beth Young (13).......................................129
Harriet Elizabeth Barnfield-Clarke (14)......130
Ellie Lousie Rutter (13).............................131
Laurie Grizzell (12)...................................132
Jessica Mason (12) 133
Kirsty Haines (12).....................................134
Anna Blaney (12) 135
Georgina Downes (12)..............................136
Jessica Skuse (12)....................................137
Abigail Morris (13) 138

Philippa Jacob (12) 139
Nicole Snipe (12) 140
Annabelle Newland (12) 141
Georgina Gibbs (12) 142
Lucy Street (12) 143
Tasmin Sanghera (12) 144
Chloe Derricutt (12) 145
Natasha Ratti (13) 146
Luze Cavelle-Lock (12) 147
Charlotte Arnold (12) 148
Phoebe Groves (12) 149
Jessica Appleton (12) 150
Charlotte Bourne (13) 151
Sophie Condlyffe (13) 152
Ellie Morriss (12) 153
Jennifer Cahill (12) 154
Anna Dowty (11) 155
Sophie Baker (13) 156
Emilia Meredith (12) 157
Victoria Weaver (13) 158
Emily Brazier (14) 159

Hijaz College, Nuneaton

Shahbaz Hassan (13) 160
Amir Shehu (15) 161

Holy Trinity School, Kidderminster

Kirtey Verma (15) 162
Rachael King (15) 163

John Kyrle High School Sixth Form College, Ross-on-Wye

Ciara Holmes (11) 164
Tasha Hughes (12) 165
Abbey Colwell (11) 166
Nikita Bagga (11) 167
Freya Jarrett (11) 168
Olivia Mace (11) 169
Rebecca Collins (11) 170
Lewis Fletcher (12) 171
Lucy Dean (11) 172
Hannah Hayes (12) 173
Emily Mince (11) 174
Aimee Stevenson (11) 175
Clare Bailey (12) 176
Luke Craig (11) 177
Lauren Darkes (11) 178
Fred Hunt (11) 179
Tanith Green (12) 180
Kim Holder (11) 181
Jack Lindley (11) 182
Emily Reynolds (11) 183

Joseph Fear (11) 184
Rebecca Gardner (12) 185

Moorside High School, Werrington

Casey Abbott (12) 186
Jordan Walker (13) 187
Thomas Hunt (12) 188
Katie Meredith (12) 189
Emma Grainger (12) 190
Beth Clews (11)..................................191
Louise Weston (11) 192
Jordan Wheeler (11) 193
Alex Lovatt (11)..................................194
Farrah Barber (12)..............................195
Sam Milward (11) 196
Chloe Warren (11) 197
Ryan Fox (12) 198
James Brindley (12)..............................199
Daniel Lowe (12)................................200
Dana Carter (13) 201
Edward Scragg (11) 202
Ben Smith (12)....................................203
Brandon Unwin (12)...........................204
Chloe Brown (12)...............................205
Samuel Bateman (13)...........................206
Ellen Thorpe (12) 207

Annie Harvey (12) 208
Jordan Botham (12) 209
Amy Bullock (12) 210
Hannah Whitehall (12)..........................211
Leah Nelson (13) 212
Nick Bourne (12).................................213
Shalon Laidler (12)...............................214
Tom Price (12) 215
Beth Trivett (12) 216
Callum Edge (12).................................217
Laura Cash (12) 218
Rebecca Littlehales (13).........................219
April Whitehurst (12) 220
Lucy Goodstadt (12).............................221
Emma Tulley (12).................................222
Kiera Fawcett (12) 223
Madeleine James (12) 224
Jordan Lander (12) 225
Robert Mapperson (11) 226
Lucy Tomkinson (12)............................227
Emily Woolley (12) 228
Lewis Adams (12).................................229

Pershore High School, Pershore

Rebecca Wheeler (17).........................230
Alex Woodman (17) 231

Elisabeth Graham (17).............................232
Katherine Green (17) 233
Melissa Creese (17),,................................234
Holly-Elizabeth Toney (13) 235
Sophie Harbridge (13) 236
Ryan Cooper (13)...................................237
Michael Wheatley (13)............................238
Emily Bitcon (14).....................................239
Rosie Bond (13).......................................240
Ryan Branfield (14)..................................241
Jared White (13).......................................242
Lauren Osborne (13)...............................243
Katie Dawson (13)...................................244
Rebecca Dawkes (17)...............................245

River House School,
Henley in Arden

Kieran Rifat (12)..246
Scott Humphries (11)...............................247
Ryan Laverty (14) 248
Lewis Coulton (14)...................................249
Brandon Curzon-Hope (12).....................250

St Mary's RC High School, Hereford

Lydia Stansbury (12) 251
Catherine Beaumont (12).........................252
Abigail Powell (11)....................................253

Millie Manning (11) 254
Rosalie Herrera-Henshaw (11)................255
Kirsty Myers (11)......................................256
Grace Rider (12).......................................257
Alice Eckley (11).......................................258
Katie Powell (11) 259
Rebecca Young (11)..................................260
Danielle Gabb (11) 261
Ross Hutchinson (11)...............................262
Kate Barber (11).......................................263
Conor Kearns (12)...................................264
Megan Shaw (11)......................................265
Owen Rogers (11).....................................266
Leah Cottrell (12).....................................267
Eleanor Brazewell (11).............................268

Sir Graham Balfour High School,
Stafford

Hassan Shariff (13)....................................269

Whitecross High School, Hereford

Emily Roantree (12)..................................270
Jessica Ruck (12).......................................271
Thomas Davies (11) 272
Richard Hancock (11)...............................273
Harry Bradbury (11).................................274
Emily Grubb (11)......................................275

Cara Powell (11)..276
Marley George (11)..................................277
Calum Loveridge (11)..............................278
Oliver Taylor (11)....................................279
Ryan Meyrick (11) 280

The Mini Sagas

Love Dream

Suzie loves James Gregory. He messes with her head. Her fingers tingle when she thinks about touching his blonde hair. Her heart races. She stays up all night imagining meeting him. She bores her friends about him. It was a lot easier when she just loved her horse Rupert Bear.

Gabrielle Green (14)

Adcote School for Girls, Shrewsbury

1

Recording

'Yeah - yes, we were doing fine the last time
you decided … we … lost the paramedic in a
crevice. The dogs went too. You can hear me
… can't you? I am sorry for the - the quality …
snowstorm we won't last long. No supplies.
Snow. Cold. Hopeless. Tell Marie I love her …'

Ophelia Gillyon (13)
Adcote School for Girls, Shrewsbury

Halloween

Witches and wizards dance about making up spells. Rats and snakes and bats wriggle and squirm. Bloody vampires, ghouls and ghosts flap about, doors bang loudly and people screech. *As black as tarmac, as orange as pumpkins, what a scary night,* thought Sam as he walked the streets on Halloween.

Georgina Mary Kennedy Welsh (13)
Adcote School for Girls, Shrewsbury

3

Death Is Danger, Don't Go Near It!

It was hard knowing she would die, such a young
girl being taken. It was time that killed this girl,
chewed her up and spat her out. There was no
joy, just a great feeling of grief filling the air. It was
like watching a skeleton, limp and so lifeless.

Molly Victoria Jones (13)
Adcote School for Girls, Shrewsbury

Faster And Faster

I could hear footsteps behind me, running faster
and faster. I looked around me frantically. I was
alone. Louder and louder, closer and closer
behind me.
'Lucie!' a voice said. 'She's going to kill you!'
I sighed and turned to follow my sister to where
my angry mother was waiting.

Elle Irving (14)
Alcester High School, Alcester

Look Behind The Frame

Looking into the wooden frame I saw an
unfamiliar face, stroking her cheek it felt like
normal glass, smiling as always, but the warm
feeling wasn't there. I saw her every day, she's
always been there. I can't believe Mum's dead and
lying in the wooden frame of her coffin.

Jessica Carter (14)

Alcester High School, Alcester

The True Danger

The turquoise water washed over his pale face, draining what little colour he had left. He was sinking deeper and deeper into the translucent water. He couldn't shout, nobody would hear his cry. He was wrong about the danger; the water was the true danger. He took his last breath.

Esther Parr (13)
Alcester High School, Alcester

7

Alone

Running at me, nothing could stop him. Not the glare of the lights or the scream in my mouth, eyes like torches in the inky darkness.
When he reached me he said, 'Nothing would stop me coming here and nothing will stop me now.' I knew it was the end.

Ally Broomfield-Gull (12)
Alcester High School, Alcester

Shadows

Darkness swallowed me whole, dragging me further into my miserable assumptions. Slowly and silently the shadow crept into sight, my fear and confusion clogging up my airways - taking my breath away like a wisp of wind on a cold morning.
Suddenly the darkness left me and the creature was gone.

Laura Giles (13)
Alcester High School, Alcester

9

Untitled

'Mum!' cried John. 'Are you hurt? What did he do to you?'

His mum could not reply as blood was pouring out of her head.

Then John's dad burst through the door and yelled. 'Ha! We fooled you!'

Then John's mum stood up and said, 'I dropped the red paint!'

Joshua Brookes (12)
Alcester High School, Alcester

Home Alone

The young child had terror and panic etched into his face. Then suddenly *knock! Knock! Knock!* He wanted to hide and cry but the courageous boy glided to the looming door. He opened the door. There stood a tall slender man in a red velvet suit.
'Trick or treat?
'Muhahahahh!'

Adam Kenyon (12)
Alcester High School, Alcester

11

The Beast!

Alan was sweating. The beast was coming towards the door. Its feet echoed in the house … the door slowly opened. It was a horrific sight, mangled hair dripping constantly (but this wasn't just a bad hair day), wrapped in dark robes! It reached to him!

'Shower's ready,' said his sister.

Timothy Bradley (13)
Alcester High School, Alcester

That One Moment Before Death

Hannah crept cautiously down the stairs, blood trailing down her hands, fingers trembling on the banister. Suddenly she saw a faint shadow of a broad man standing behind her, still and cold. 'I've been waiting all my life for this,' he said in a deep voice and stabbed her.

Laura Willcox (12)

Alcester High School, Alcester

The Tale Of The Corpse Bride

Emily was getting married to a grim man but her
daddy said no so they decided to run away.
She was ready, where was he? She sat down
surrounded by trees waiting for him.
The man came and committed a murderer most
foul. So she became a corpse bride.

Emily Sabin (12)
Alcester High School, Alcester

Merry Christmas

'Merry Christmas,' said Andrew as he entered
the room. Opening up his present in front of him,
'What's this?' he said disappointed.
'It's a yo-yo.'
His face was burning with rage. 'I wanted a blue
one *not* red!' he said.

Jason Batts (12)
Alcester High School, Alcester

The Washing

Tom's hands were sweaty as he hung another
peg. He screamed in surprise as a creature landed
on the back of his neck, he swiped out.
'Tom,' his mum called, 'There's a fly on your back
and hurry up with the washing, it's going to rain.'

Josh Godson (12)

Alcester High School, Alcester

The Phone Call

The phone rang. It made me and everyone else in the room freeze in motion. This had happened twice already. Every time no one knowing what would be said. I answered, knowing this phone call could change my life or end it. Then he asked me, 'Deal or no deal?'

Ben Wiltshire (15)
Alcester High School, Alcester

17

On The Edge

Stood on the edge of the roof, Jack started to regret his decisions. He shouldn't be there. He edged forward, started to tip, falling gracefully, finally at peace. He rapidly made contact with the ground, a loud sickening crunch. The scene devastating.

'Cut!' shouted the director. 'Someone remove the dummy.'

James Reeves (14)
Alcester High School, Alcester

Horror At Home!

I was not alone. A dark presence surrounded me. I was being closed in by something I could no longer see. Suddenly a sharp cold wind rushed down my spine. I was falling, down, down, down I went.

Then all of a sudden I woke up! It was a nightmare.

Marianne Hoy (15)
Alcester High School, Alcester

19

Jigsaw Puzzle

The game began. I searched the house for the final piece of the puzzle, so many had failed before me.

There it was, wedged between the dusty floorboards. I obtained it and ran, time running out. I slotted it in and screamed with joy. I had beaten the 'Kittens' jigsaw!

Luis Sone (15)

Alcester High School, Alcester

The Screaming Girl

People coughed. Sickness surrounded every
chair. 'Argh! Stop! Stop! It hurts!' They held her
down so she couldn't move.
'Please, no, it's so long.'
He started to get annoyed now as five minutes
had passed.
'Look, this won't hurt if you calm down. Settle.
Good. Now for the tetanus jab.'

Andrew Ward (14)

Alcester High School, Alcester

21

The Shadow

Chloe walked down the alleyway, the only light flickering. She could barely see. A figure dashed in front of her, the shadow resting on the pavement. She ran through the cold night air, not looking back.

Reaching the house, she locked the door when a voice whispered, 'You're not alone …'

Ellie Muitt (14)

Alcester High School, Alcester

Fear Of Dying

She fell to the ground, as she was pushed from
behind. An evil laugh rippled through the air. Her
blood ran down her face onto the ground. He
leant down, his lips brushing against her ear. Her
heart was pounding as the fear of dying set into
her heart.

'Mine!'

Charlotte Tudberry (13)

Alcester High School, Alcester

23

Cliff Hanger

'Help!' yelled Bob as he dangled from the cliff
face. A passer-by called the fire brigade and they
arrived shortly.

'We'll get you up!' exclaimed the fire-fighter
frantically. The fire-fighters lifted the man to
safety.

'Oh thank you. Let me reward you with lunch, I
was about to eat, mate.'

Samuel Bevins (13)

Alcester High School, Alcester

The Escape

As I reluctantly walked towards the door, it slowly creaked open. I carried on walking, getting even more scared as I approached.
I entered the house. The door slammed shut behind me. It made my heart jump out my skin! 'You're mine now!' a creepy voice cackled. I must escape!

Christian Rushton (14)
Alcester High School, Alcester

25

The Light That Flickered

The door creaked open. From the corner of my eye, I saw a candle flicker. Then footsteps got closer, *click, clock*. Suddenly everything went silent, no light, no footsteps, no breathing. It was quiet for one minute when I heard a breath in the room …then another in my ear …

Chiara Plotegher (14)
Alcester High School, Alcester

Dream Rider

As he thunders into the lead, Ron exhales deeply.
He looks back to check Byzantium's footing. Ron
leans further to get a closer look at the chestnut
thoroughbred's slender legs. Suddenly his foot
slips out of the iron and he begins to fall …
drumming hooves trample Ron's dreams to dust.

Isabel Smith (14)
Alcester High School, Alcester

On The Run

She must keep running. They are coming for her.
Her breath comes out in uneven pants, every
bone in her body screams in protest. The eerily
lit streets illuminate her face, red with effort. The
footsteps behind her are getting closer. There is
nothing she can do. They are coming …

Rebecca Mottram (13)
Alcester High School, Alcester

Attack On The Aircraft

Boom! A shot was fired in the back of the aircraft.
I sprang from my seat and dashed to the cockpit.
A muscular man had an AK47 in his hand. Quickly
I grabbed the gun and elbowed him in the back of
the head. He dropped down.

Jake Williams (14)
Alcester High School, Alcester

29

Winter Murderer

It was a frosty morning. Katie was walking on the crispy snow to school. There was a man with a black hoodie on. He had a knife. Katie quickly hid behind a tree. Slipping on the crystal-white snow the monster stabbed someone.
Ten years later she hasn't told anyone …

Emma Garrett (13)

Alcester High School, Alcester

On The Bike

I am on the motorbike, dirt splatters everywhere.
My cheeks are squished from inside my helmet.
I'm coming up to the jump. My heart is racing so
fast. This is a big one. I give it full power. I glance
behind me. Yes, I've cleared the jump! Great
track!

Morgan Alcock (13)
Alcester High School, Alcester

The Path In The Wood

The path got narrower as she carried on running. The trees started to blow a gale; she could hear footsteps getting closer behind her. She didn't look back, she headed for the opening of the wood where she could see the sun setting. The scream echoed throughout the deserted wood …

Beth Radbourne (14)

Alcester High School, Alcester

The Quest

The darkness enveloped the final destination of
his quest. Nowhere could hide itself from it, it
was everywhere. No life could be detected, only
the cobwebs hanging loosely from the walls. But
nothing could stop him, he reached in ...
'Billy, have you found your teddy?'
'Yes Mum,' he replied, triumphantly.

Bryn Sanford (13)
Alcester High School, Alcester

The Beast

I pulled out the gleaming knife, slicing through
the flesh of the beast. Hitting the bone my knife
halts. The juices are pouring out. Pulling off one of
the legs, I bite into it, the meat is nice and easy to
get from the bone.
'Um, this is nice turkey.'

Zak Gavin (14)

Alcester High School, Alcester

Rudolph The Red-Nosed Reindeer

Santa rode his sleigh in the dark every Christmas
night so when Rudolph came along it was an
outstanding sight. The other reindeers disagreed
and simply said there was no need. But that night
they saw the sky and the stars that passed by, that
night, that outstanding night.

Molly Malin (13)
Alcester High School, Alcester

The Sleepwalker

Lo, behold the sleeper walks! She walks, eyes closed, without a flaw. She's fast asleep and yet she writes a page-long letter every night. The simple reason for all that, she killed the king and that is that! Beware she's no sweet flower. She'll kill for power!

Nina Gunton (12)

Alcester High School, Alcester

The Death Of Lady Macbeth

The light was fading, there was a deathly silence. Something was up or maybe down? A large thudding sound rippled through the still air around me. I heard the scream from the window at the top of the tower. The bone-crunching thud confirmed my worst fears, it had happened …

Alexander Cox (13)

Alcester High School, Alcester

37

The Girl Who Gets Lost In Time

It was stormy, the trees outside were making scary figures. Amy curled up under her duvet and shook, scared and alone. Meanwhile a portal was whizzing through time to catch the unexpected. A flash of light awoke Amy Rose and captured her to take her somewhere she'd never been before.

Hannah Clury (12)

Alcester High School, Alcester

The Man

It was dark. I was in an alley when a man in the
shadows attacked me. He pulled out a knife. I
started to run but he was quicker. I hid but he
found me. I caught a glimpse of his half-mutilated
face with a missing eye …
I woke!

Ben Godson (12)
Alcester High School, Alcester

Arrgghh!

It darted, swerved and vanished. The bed was quivering and respiring though nothing was there. All of a sudden she felt a breeze on her neck and was startled. After having been shocked she pegged it down the stairs and huddled up on the sofa. The sofa started to wobble …

Laura Smith (14)
Alcester High School, Alcester

The Best Pies In Town

She dropped what she was carrying. A boy looked closer at what she was carrying. There was a hand! In shock the boy leapt to his feet and ran as far as he could. He felt so sick after realising he'd just eaten a human!

Georgia Buxton (14)
Alcester High School, Alcester

41

A Trip To The Barbers

The shadow crept towards me. A blade shone in the light. A razor buzzed at me. Fear struck me. A voice said, 'Are you ready?' I slowly shuffled to the door hoping to escape. The light beamed. There he was, the blade glinting in the light. The barber approached …

Jack Baker (13)
Alcester High School, Alcester

The Shiny Blade

I sat stiff in the chair, scared. He pulled open a
drawer, I saw the razor. Its blade was sharp like
cut glass. He lifted it to my head.
'How short do you want your hair then?'

Katherine Hudson (13)

Alcester High School, Alcester

43

The Dreaded House

The crooked house towered over me. I reached out to the lion-faced knocker. My fingertips gripped around the circular knocker, *knock, knock*. Fear ran through my body and I took a deep breath. The door swung open. A large lady stood there.

'Welcome to your new school, Katie.'

Mollie-Anne Shepherd (13)

Alcester High School, Alcester

The Monster

It was here again. The monster stepped inside, ready to take its next victim. The young girl stared, fear noticeable in her eyes. The monster took one more step forward, making the floorboard creak.

'Hello,' he said, his voice low and threatening. 'Hello Dad,' whispered the girl. Terror had arrived.

Caroline Stewart (13)
Alcester High School, Alcester

The Race

Broom! Two cars raced against each other battling for victory. Colourful vehicles rapidly dashed from left to right. A competitive rider drove his engine of speed whilst cheering words of encouragement. *Crash!*

'Timmy! I told you to be careful with those toy cars. We've just had the new carpet fitted!'

Nicole Clay-Noonan (13)
Alcester High School, Alcester

Little Red Riding Hood

Once upon a day, a young girl breathed carrying a
basket, she struggled, she heaved.
Her old nan said, 'My darling what's wrong?' She
was tired, stressed, the day felt so long. She left
the cottage, feeling much better but not long after
I heard the wolf got her!

Bethan Leahy (12)
Alcester High School, Alcester

Untitled

Am I obsessed? The word 'love' runs through my head. Is this 'the one?' Am I sad to pretend to have a conversation with him in my mirror because I'm too scared at school? I guess I can try but he won't be interested. He won't like ugly me.

Leah Ballinger (13)
Alcester High School, Alcester

Angry Flames

Tracy stayed deathly still, never taking her eyes
off the angry flickering flames. She could feel the
sharp burning feeling flickering over her nose. Her
eyes got wider as the flames grew stronger.
'Happy birthday,' screamed her family and
friends as Tracy extinguished the flames from her
birthday cake candles.

Natalie Price (14)
Alcester High School, Alcester

49

Untitled

He ran deeper and deeper into the house. The shadow was approaching. He pulled his gun and fired a warning shot, but it was too late, the shadow disappeared from view … He felt a warm breath on the back of the neck, he instantly froze, a horrific scream arose … silence.

Max Tarrant (13)

Alcester High School, Alcester

Untitled

Fear, catastrophe filled the atmosphere. The young mouse ran from his predator. Beads of perspiration formed on his head. All he was to another animal was lunch. His determination to live was overwhelming. He manoeuvred around the room, avoiding the obstacles, and the predator! Luckily the mouse survived … for today!

Jerome Bailey (13)
Bristnall Hall Technology College, Oldbury

She's Gone

She's gone, I can't believe it. She was the best, I'll miss her. All the times we went to those places, Devon, France, the city of romance, Paris. I loved her so much. She's only been here since 1993. She went too soon. She's the best car I've ever had.

Callum Cleary (12)
Bristnall Hall Technology College, Oldbury

I'm Flying In The Air

We took off. *I'm on the way to Spain,* I thought.
There were lots of other people also going to
Spain. I could feel the wind, literally. We landed;
I ate some seeds off the ground. The other
birds finally landed, including my family. I was so
relieved they did.

Alex Sandhu (12)

Bristnall Hall Technology College, Oldbury

53

My Puppy

Bounding, flopping, leaping through leaves has
not a care in the world. Whining, howling, barking
loud, shedding hairs all over the brand new rug.
Running, sliding, claws digging, the lawn looks
atrocious with crater-like holes. Sighing, yawning,
head nodding, he curls up in his small, fluffy bed,
my puppy!

Phoebe Hinton-Sheley (13)
Bristnall Hall Technology College, Oldbury

Concentration Of Winning

Hearts beating and steady hands, I hold my
breath, grasping the handle with the energy I have
left. The fear gets to me, the metal collides, the
sweat drips off my forehead the buzzer goes, just
inches from completion. The steady hand game
was nearly completed, maybe next time.

Aiden Ashton (13)

Bristnall Hall Technology College, Oldbury

The Knock!

I sat on the sofa watching the television. It was late; suddenly there was a bang on the window. It couldn't be him. I had visions of that night over again. I walked up to the window, my heart was pounding! I pulled back the curtain … it was the police!

Amber Marshall (12)

Bristnall Hall Technology College, Oldbury

Jack The Ripper And The Darkest Abyss

A woman is darting down a dark corridor. Jack the Ripper closely follows, he is wearing a black trench coat and carrying knives in both hands. She gets to the door as he throws both knives, they closely miss her. He finally catches her and takes her into the abyss.

Ryan Colledge (13)
Bristnall Hall Technology College, Oldbury

57

Alone In A Cell

They torture me. They give me headaches.
I think it was a big mistake. No breaks, no
freedom, no fun, no love and no time alone.
Constantly they watch me, always they hurt me.
I'm now suffering pain in silence. I can't wait until
I'm out. My frightening cell guards.

Rowena Ellis (12)

Bristnall Hall Technology College, Oldbury

Growth

Dark, warm and moist; that was my home. I was
happy there until one day, I cracked. Long green
things grew from my head. What was happening
to me? I got taller and taller until light burned my
eyes. It was horrible. I knew I was changing.
What am I?

Jessica Clews (12)

Bristnall Hall Technology College, Oldbury

59

3D Disaster

They all sit back, everything is silent. Just like
a row of dominoes, one will jump then they'll
all start. A piercing scream's heard, then one
says, 'Calm down.' A knife comes towards
them, they've started shaking. Now the movie is
finished someone says, '3D horror movies actually
feel real!'

Emily Parsons (12)

Bristnall Hall Technology College, Oldbury

Lost At Sea

Waves crashing against the frail old wooden boat,
the paint being washed off as if it is running away.
The oars have been lost at sea, unfortunately, so
will the men stranded aboard. As before they can
call for help, the sea will deliver them into the
hands of death.

Katie McCarron (12)

Bristnall Hall Technology College, Oldbury

61

Taken Away

Lifted from a bright room with plants, slowly taken to a room full of people rushing around and going in and out. Placed on a plank of wood lying there for someone to come back and help. Slowly dying, hoping for someone to take me home. Please, someone help me!

Matthew Gibson (12)

Bristnall Hall Technology College, Oldbury

New Life Today

New life's come today out in a field big, green and
very, very lush. Our shiny, fresh red faces grow
all around. Never leaving, people can pick us
every year on our colour shape and size. We are a
symbol to remember the people who died here.
The poppy field.

Heather Frear (12)
Bristnall Hall Technology College, Oldbury

It Happened So Fast

He sat. He smiled, sarcastically. The cup of tea sitting on a tray was slowly going cold. Waiting. Time wasn't going by fast. His 'smile' was fading as the room got gloomier. The cup of tea fell onto his lap. Something wasn't right. The plane was going lower. Darkness approached …

Katie Nikolic (13)

Bristnall Hall Technology College, Oldbury

The Chop

As I was walking down the road I heard a loud chop. I kept on walking, trying to forget the noise then another. I walked towards the sound. Then I saw a large grey object closing in on a large piece of meat, on a family dinner table one Sunday.

Jonathan Davies (12)

Bristnall Hall Technology College, Oldbury

Burnt Alive!

I lie down with my family in a soft comfortable place. Suddenly, a cold object grabs me and places me in a tray; an obscure machine turns it on. Hotness! I'm on my own in here. All I can hear is a loud humming noise until … *pop!* I'm toast.

Beth Henderson (12)

Bristnall Hall Technology College, Oldbury

66

Typical Mistake

The light flicks off. I hear *drip, drip, drip*.
Footsteps surround me; slowly I walk to the
bathroom. The dripping gets louder and louder.
I'm getting closer. As I enter the room; a cold
hand strikes my shoulder. I scream. The light flicks
on … it is my big sister Jodie.

Harriet Hynes (12)
Bristnall Hall Technology College, Oldbury

Hanging On

I am here, stuck to a branch. The wind blowing against me, I feel myself falling away from the branch; my home! I sway with the wind, left to right. The ground is getting nearer. I gently fall onto the grassy bed, it's comfy and soft. I am a leaf.

Clare Gardner (12)

Bristnall Hall Technology College, Oldbury

Shadow ...

Out of the shadows and into the light, quietly
creeping towards me. Backing away, tiptoeing
carefully, trying not to make a sound. Coming
closer towards me and getting bigger every step
of the way, with my back facing against the wall
there is nowhere to run from it ...

Aneesa Malik (13)
Bristnall Hall Technology College, Oldbury

One Way Trip

It was so crowded, yet isolated to me. A riot was brewing yet I fell silent. I sat, still as stone whilst people walked past, coming and going. It was all nothing to me. All I could do was wait until my time would come to leave the bus stop.

Dalton Cooper (12)

Bristnall Hall Technology College, Oldbury

Untitled

I ran fast, the cold was whistling across my face,
my hair dragging behind me, it felt like it was
dragging me backwards. My heart was pounding,
nearly there but I only had thirty seconds to get
there.
OK, just round the corner. No! It was going, I'd
missed it.

Taylor Bromley (12)
Bristnall Hall Technology College, Oldbury

71

The Daily Struggle

The daily struggle. As the light shines in, staying still, motionless, arguing with myself. Thinking, *shall I?* But no movement. Legs, arms, head, body, stuck, unable to move. Trying to avoid the struggle of imprisonment. The daily struggle not being able to get up for school. I'll be late again.

Melissa Limbrick (13)

Bristnall Hall Technology College, Oldbury

Terrorised Walk

There I was, surrounded by scum and terror; the odds against me were very bad. I thought to myself, *I'm going to die here, I'm gonna be slaughtered.* Then a brainwave hit, there was a secret door round the corner. I ran as fast as I could. I stumbled over ...

Alex Smith (12)

Bristnall Hall Technology College, Oldbury

73

Nervous Breakdown

I was blinded from the crowd, lights were flashing in my face. Buzzing was in my ear. I was a nervous wreck. I went to say my line, it got all muddled up! I tried to imagine them in their underwear.
The bell finally went and assembly had finally ended!

Jodie Davis (12)

Bristnall Hall Technology College, Oldbury

Silent Screams

In the corner silently waiting, no one to hear
my screams. The crying and the screeching,
the punching and the kicking, the torture. I am
coming to the end of my road. But with a creak
and a crack, the light bursts through… I've
reached my destination. I'm at school.

Elise Caddick (12)
Bristnall Hall Technology College, Oldbury

The Rubbish Dump

Once again I picked up the same old rubbish,
folding my trousers, picking up smelly shoes.
The bear slide tumbled down onto me. Suddenly
a secret door came out of nowhere. My hand
trembled. I left it. Back to the beginning, picking
up the same old rubbish. My bedroom.

Dionne Bailey (12)
Bristnall Hall Technology College, Oldbury

Useless

Finally, out. A frightening thing lifts me from the darkened room. As the monster squashes me my blood runs onto the white surface, forming some symbols. Slowly dying, becoming useless. I hear shouting. So pretty before, so nice and kind; now I am an empty pen that nobody wants.

Dominika Pietrak (12)

Bristnall Hall Technology College, Oldbury

Out Of Touching Distance

Strolling into the moon-filled night, Billy was oblivious to the dark devil looming just inches away. *Thud* and a *bang!* The sky was spiralling round, echoing birds, the luminous beast floated away. Sleek as a panther into the now drowned but still gaping backdrop of the winter's night.

Brett Huxley (14)

Bromsgrove School, Bromsgrove

Awkward

The night sky was filled with sparkling stars and the atmosphere calm. As we lay there, all the worries of that day were lost and in his soft gentle romantic voice. He whispered in my ear, 'I love you.'
At that moment his wife appeared, 'You weasel, cheating on me!'

Laura-May Matthews (15)
Bromsgrove School, Bromsgrove

79

The Creep

Fiery and angry, strong and mad, she lies in wait,
smiling gently.
One day, when all else sleeps, mountains steep,
the sparrows cheep. She will creep, not sleep.
The cold finger plays on them like ice. Fiery and
angry, strong and mad, she lies waiting snorting,
only to passers-by.

James Lay (15)
Bromsgrove School, Bromsgrove

Humanity

A glint of metal swishing through the air, a blade,
slipping into flesh. Metallic screams begin to
rise, falling into emptiness, into darkness. A pool
forming from drips upon the floor, the blood
turning to ice upon the floor. Stillness in the dark.
This story is that of your humanity.

James Hey (15)
Bromsgrove School, Bromsgrove

On The Run!

I could hear him, he wasn't far behind us now.
I felt nothing but pure fear, my heart was in my
mouth. I grabbed my mother's trembling hand
and cried out, 'Why's that man chasing us?'
'He wants to kill us darling.'
Gobsmacked, I replied, 'Why?'
There was no reply …

Sophie Haycock-Jones (14)
Bromsgrove School, Bromsgrove

Untitled

A lady of romance, her toes touch the crest of
the wave as it hits the shore, her hair so golden.
She notices a shadow. A shadow not of attitude,
but of beauty, of nature. She has not fallen for this
stranger but for her closest partner. The beaming
sun.

Thomas Gretton (14)
Bromsgrove School, Bromsgrove

83

Doctor Adrian

Grey was the day, the rain was limp and weak.
Adrian looked at his patient, sick and infantile. His
clipboard showed his deepest dread. His face,
gaunt and grey like this rainy day.
'I'm sorry Sir, there's nothing we can do.' It was
going to be another long grey day.

Sam Coope (14)
Bromsgrove School, Bromsgrove

The Shooting

He clenched the handle with his sweaty palm and with his index finger he forced the trigger back. *Bang!* The bullet exploded out of the gun and flew through the crisp night air. The bullet drove into the cold pale skin of the innocent unsuspecting victim and stabbed his heart.

Rachel Clare (14)

Bromsgrove School, Bromsgrove

The Beginning Of The End

It was late, midnight, black outside the window.
He tied her to the chair, furiously. Everything he
said was a lie, he didn't mean a word of it, love?
Her friends had warned her, and now look what
it'd come to. Knife to her throat, the beginning of
the end …

Emma Rowell (13)
Bromsgrove School, Bromsgrove

Rebirth

The ashes stirred in the wind's breath, then
swirled and twisted in the air, revealing the image
of a teenage boy. He blinked. Gossamer wings
sprang out behind him. He took a deep breath;
golden flames enclosing his whole being. The
wings flapped once; the boy leaped. Phoenix was
reborn.

Sam Adamson (13)

Bromsgrove School, Bromsgrove

Goodbye

Her warm, soothing breath rolled quietly across his face as the crimson curtains blew across her naked body. 'Don't leave me here, Johnny.'
'I have no choice, but I will return to marry you when the war is over.'
They dressed silently, knowing that their time together was nearly over.

George Goucher (13)
Bromsgrove School, Bromsgrove

Untitled

I was in the coliseum, surrounded by roaring,
screeching Romans. Then the lion was on me.
Its face curled in a deep growl. Its yellow teeth,
dripping with blood. I picked up a dusty spear and
hurled it at the beast. It swerved and lunged at
me, sharp claws out …

Sam Rose (13)
Bromsgrove School, Bromsgrove

The End

She heard the door creak open and the rush of the wind whistle past her. Her tanned complexion flushed to a pale ghost-line figure, then a distant wail of distress came from the door. Her mother rushed to the entrance as soon as her daughter collapsed. She stared memorised, silently.

Stephanie Swatkins (13)
Bromsgrove School, Bromsgrove

Bouquet From A Boy!

I received some flowers today. They were glowing red roses. They made me blush but a thorn made me bleed. They were from a boy twice my age. My parents say he is from the wrong side of the tracks but then, that is the side I am on too!

Bethan Luckman (13)
Bromsgrove School, Bromsgrove

Love

The couple stared at the sun setting over the sea … memories flooded back. It was here he had first taken her hand all those years ago. She turned to him, smiling, the sun glowing on her wrinkled face. No words were necessary as she quietly slipped her hand in his.

Carliene Silk (13)

Bromsgrove School, Bromsgrove

Black Hole

Two huge fangs tore holes in the front of the spacecraft. Oxygen gushed out of the hull. But how could this horrific beast have survived a black hole? Minutes earlier they had watched it vanish into the abyss. One by one the monster was devouring the crew, who was next?

Alexander Berwick (13)

Bromsgrove School, Bromsgrove

Bloody Murder

A piercing scream emanated from the kitchen.
My hands were clammy. I was breathing hard;
too hard. Could they hear me? I glanced around
the corner, blood was splattered up the wall. A
masked figure looked up and froze. I screamed as
his bloody axe embedded itself into my flesh.

Amy Foster (13)
Bromsgrove School, Bromsgrove

Blood On The Tiles

As Daniel rounded the corner, his heart stopped.
A huge man with pale, chalk-like skin stood in
Daniel's kitchen, holding a bloodied axe, dripping
on the pearl-white tiles. A foul stench gushed
from his mouth. The next and last thing Daniel
knew was an axe flying towards him …

Asher Hardy (14)
Bromsgrove School, Bromsgrove

Untitled

Warm, salty tears rolled down my ashen face. My heart frantically beating as the train disappeared and my sense of loss and fear was unbearable. Cruelty of war kept my life on hold until that dreaded knock. A cold formal telegram bearing my husband's name, my beloved now a memory.

Abbie-May Griffiths (14)
Bromsgrove School, Bromsgrove

Deep Void

Violent shudders ran through the hulls of the
dying warship as the Torgan's cannon ripped
through deck after deck of the drastically
weakening ship.
The captain brought up his multi-screen to
contact the mid-shipman down in engineering
only to see his own crippled ship and the void of
space …

Matthew Budge (13)

Bromsgrove School, Bromsgrove

97

The Coin Journey

He was sitting all alone on the bench, people
walking past, backwards and forwards, purposely
ignoring him. All he had was a coin in his hands
which a man had given him earlier.
'What is it, what does it do?'
He got up and started his journey.

Andrea Ellins (13)

Bromsgrove School, Bromsgrove

Untitled

She hurried through the silent, empty forest; he
had abandoned her life force, her mind controlled
by love, her life swallowed up by his presence.
How would she ever get away? Where could she
escape to? There was nowhere to run, the path
was disappearing. Was this the end?

Montana Bent (14)
Bromsgrove School, Bromsgrove

I Can't Explain. Oh, Wait! No, Still Can't

Explanation, that's my aim. You see I'm being
possessed by my own indulgence. However
heartbreaking it seems, please, please don't slow
me down. I know you're not boring, so don't
deceive yourself. Explanation is my aim, but
release is my outcome. Even though I keep trying
I still cannot explain.

George Toft
Bromsgrove School, Bromsgrove

Untitled

There it was, the most magnificent sight possible.
With skin that shone like a star slowly falling
into the palm of my hand. I paused, closed my
eyes, opened, and it was gone. I looked up at
the freezing cold drop upon my cheek, it was
beautiful, it was snowing.

Edward Philp (15)
Bromsgrove School, Bromsgrove

Fearless

The beast was looking at me with its red eyes
drilling through me, but it could not find any fear.
Impossible, it thought. *Why does he not fear?*
Simply because I knew I was stronger. I knew I
would win. I'd lost before, but this time I would
win!

Ivan Taptygin (14)
Bromsgrove School, Bromsgrove

Aid Of The Soldier

In corrosive mists of war, a soldier's worthiest
friends are his feet. These feet help them achieve,
and support them when they've failed to achieve.
These feet help carry those who've lost their
own, and make ashes of death's fire. And these
are the feet that will bring them home.

Calum Cooper (14)
Bromsgrove School, Bromsgrove

Will It Catch Us?

We ran as fast as we could. Twisting, turning through the trees it was gaining on us. It made a leap on us and caught us. We were pinned to the floor; it was ripping us apart and eating us. Then the titles came on and we ejected the DVD.

Emmeline Charlotte Trenchard-Mole (12)

Dodderhill School, Droitwich Spa

The Disappointment

I was so excited! I'd been waiting so long. This was the moment I'd waited for! My heart was thumping dramatically. This was it.
But then, 'I'm so sorry, we don't have your size but we have your size in other colours.'
'Oh well, it doesn't matter.'

Olivia Cox (11)

Dodderhill School, Droitwich Spa

The Furry Thing At The Window

One day I was looking through the window and saw a furry thing. It was grey-black. It started to move. It had a tail, it had whiskers and two green eyes watching me, and two pointed ears, very pink inside. I knew it was my cat. Sorry, Tab.

Alexandra Stephenson (11)
Dodderhill School, Droitwich Spa

The Wedding

Sally was just about to say, 'I do,' when Tom
burst in and told her he loved her. Sally looked at
Nick and said, 'I am so sorry.' She threw the ring
on the floor and ran off with Tom. So that's all you
missed on EastEnders.

Katie Edgington (12)
Dodderhill School, Droitwich Spa

The Hunt

It moved quickly through the long grass, not making any sound. It moved graciously while stalking its prey. Its bright green eyes dazzled, its patterned fur shimmered in the light. Nothing could distract it from catching its prey. It got ready to pounce … the cat pounced on the mouse.

Phoebe Clayton (12)
Dodderhill School, Droitwich Spa

Drowning

My head was then underwater which was going up my nose. My eyes were stinging, I swallowed a mouthful of water. It was making me choke and then I pulled my head out of the sink and dried it on the warm soft towel.

Isobel Fox (12)

Dodderhill School, Droitwich Spa

What A Dream

Sweeping through the trees having magical
powers. Stopping cars we thought it was going to
bite us. Swooping so fast we couldn't see. Only
flashes of light. It jumped …
We woke up to find the cat on top of us.

Shannon Holly Stowe (11)
Dodderhill School, Droitwich Spa

My Destiny

As I entered the ring, I couldn't catch my breath. I was about to ride my horse, Destiny, over the world's biggest jump. My nerves were getting the better of me. I'd brushed Destiny really well before but now I didn't know if he would make it over the jump.

Micayla Fradd (11)
Dodderhill School, Droitwich Spa

111

Mistaken Identity?

'Sophie, doesn't that look like Bonnie?'
'Yes, my dear. It says here Miss Bonnie and Sylvia
Green have escaped from an orphanage in West
London. If you see them please take them to your
local police station.'
'Bonnie and Sylvia aren't orphans!' growled Sir
Willoughby. 'We need to rescue them!'

Felicity Smith-Maxwell (11)
Dodderhill School, Droitwich Spa

Easter Excitement

It was Easter and I was going to get lots of chocolate Easter eggs. I kept on asking Mum why I hadn't got any yet.

She said, 'You have asked me this three times today, it's six weeks until Easter. You won't get any until five weeks is up, OK!'

Emma Bridges (11)
Dodderhill School, Droitwich Spa

The Small Saga Of Noughts And Crosses

Sephy and I had only wanted to be together but now I had been shot up to Heaven and yanked down to Hell. I hope she keeps our beautiful child and tells him or her about me. I hope that she will get on in life and not struggle alone.

Hannah Jones (11)

Dodderhill School, Droitwich Spa

The Beach

The children were walking along the beach when one of them decided to dig a big hole. Whilst they were digging they came across something very peculiar, they wondered what it was. One of them suggested that they were dinosaur bones. It turned out it was just a dead fish.

Emily Meredith (11)
Dodderhill School, Droitwich Spa

The Ghost

'What's that sound?' stammered Katie.
'I'm not sure, I can hear something in the bush,' I
replied.
We walked slowly and suddenly something
jumped out, a pale shape.
'Argh! It's a ghost,' shrieked Katie.
'No!' I cried. I pulled the shape off. 'Dad! Dad!' I
remonstrated.
'Happy Halloween,' he shouted.

Alice Fish (11)

Dodderhill School, Droitwich Spa

Trick Not Treat

'Trick or treat?' chorused ghosts and ghoulies
filling plastic pumpkins with candy. I watched their
faces break into gap-toothed grins.
'Thanks,' murmured a little witch.
'Make sure you share them around,' I said.
'Mmm,' she answered and left.
Later, I saw a face at the window. It was her …

Eleanor Kinsman (12)
Dodderhill School, Droitwich Spa

117

The Beast

The villagers crowded into the corner, trying to back away from the snarling beast which was swiping with huge clawed paws. Its eyes, as crimson as blood, were fixed on one man - the man who had stolen his life. The creature stared at the man. Revenge was approaching very swiftly.

Isabelle Palmer (12)

Dodderhill School, Droitwich Spa

Piscine Victory

Something plunged the boy into the water.
Gasping for air, he sank slowly. Something was
swirling, coiling round his feet. He looked down,
couldn't make out the creature but it was long
and thin. The boy frantically kicked out at it, he
felt innumerable creatures round him, tasting his
flesh.

Georgina Reece (11)
Dodderhill School, Droitwich Spa

Based On Romeo And Juliet

There were two families, Capulets and Montagues. Two teens in love, Romeo and Juliet, but their love was forbidden by their own parents. They met in secret, hiding. They dreamed of being able to be together, hoping that day would come. That didn't happen, so they took their own lives.

Molly Everitt (13)
Dodderhill School, Droitwich Spa

Stranded

The day was sweltering, sun shining intensely.
The blazing sand radiated across his face.
Ponderously moving across the melting sand
dunes hoping that he was heading towards an
oasis in Egypt. A clamorous noise in the distance
alerted him. He tentatively approached but to his
astonishment it was a sphinx.

Matilda Hallett (13)

Dodderhill School, Droitwich Spa

The One

My mind swam; I looked into his luscious chocolate eyes and felt like I had touched Heaven! He was the one, but who was he? Abruptly my dream was shattered as a gorgeous woman walked up to him, gave him an explosive kiss and led him out of my life.

Paige Conlon (13)
Dodderhill School, Droitwich Spa

Untitled

In a palace far far away it was Christmas. The
young mother's baby was due. She was hoping to
have it on Christmas Day.
Sure enough she had her beautiful baby on
Christmas Day. She was going to call it Angel. Her
family were there to greet her beautiful angel.

Rebecca Hardy (13)
Dodderhill School, Droitwich Spa

She Remains With Me Always

It's two years since she died. That day will remain with me forever. The sight of her closing her eyes and drawing in her last breath haunts me. She's still here, one star stands out at night, I know it's her, watching from above, sparkling like her eyes used to.

Lydia Tainty (13)
Dodderhill School, Droitwich Spa

The Toy Box

At night, when the house is dark, and the clock
strikes twelve the toy box opens. Gradually the
contents come alive. Teddy has fallen in love with
the doll. He dreams of talking to her.
The next day as it closes, the toys see them
walking towards it, linking arms.

Abigail Smith (13)
Dodderhill School, Droitwich Spa

The Smoke House

I can't see a thing. It's sweltering. Where's my friend? Is she trapped in the heat? What is that smell? It's getting harder for me to breathe. Will I survive long enough for them to come and get me? They are here, joining me in the steam room.

Emily Webster (14)

Dodderhill School, Droitwich Spa

When The Scream Came

As she wandered through the house a sudden
ear-splitting scream was heard. She ran
downstairs, terrified. All rooms were tentatively
checked. Reaching the kitchen, all she could see
was the blood of her sister, lying motionless. The
knife loomed in front of her. Nothing now; only
still, cold death.

Amelia Clancy (13)
Dodderhill School, Droitwich Spa

Driving To London On A Foggy Morning

The fog was thickening - I was getting scared!
My eyes were blurred. I couldn't see. There were
horns honking at me. Help! What to do? I stopped
the car, jumped out and found I could see. It was
steam on the windscreen! I had forgotten to put
the blower on!

Heidi Fellows (14)
Dodderhill School, Droitwich Spa

Remembering

She walked into the school playground. It was empty. She stopped and looked around. Where was everybody? She went towards the front door and looked through the windows! It was pitch-black inside. She was scared and worried. Where were her best friends?
Then she remembered, it was the weekend!

Beth Young (13)
Dodderhill School, Droitwich Spa

Follower

I ran as fast as my feet would take me. I turned
and saw him following me. I leapt onto the wall
and began to feel safe but I could feel his breath
on my shoulder. I dived through the door.
The pop-up appeared on screen. Yes! High score!

Harriet Elizabeth Barnfield-Clarke (14)

Dodderhill School, Droitwich Spa

The Gorilla

As I was watching out of my bedroom I saw a gorilla. The gorilla prowled through the streets, he stole everyone's sweets and gobbled them down. I didn't dare go outside. He had sharp claws on his big feet and a hairy chest. No, it was only Dad!

Ellie Lousie Rutter (13)
Dodderhill School, Droitwich Spa

Riding In The Woods

Riding through the woods, I heard a strange sound. I stopped, looked round but couldn't see anything. The horse bolted, there was something wrong. I ignored her, trotted on, she reared. I fell but wasn't hurt. I got back up and cantered on. I didn't hear anything. All was quiet.

Laurie Grizzell (12)

Dodderhill School, Droitwich Spa

The Hunter - Based On Greek Mythology

Long ago lived a hunter. He was brilliant. He
thought he was better than the goddess of
hunting. She heard and challenged him. They
hunted all day then counted their kills. The
goddess won. The man's skin went hard; she
turned him into an arrow and shot him into
infinity.

Jessica Mason (12)

Dodderhill School, Droitwich Spa

The End Of Life

Kerry sat in the living room watching the news.
She screamed when she saw the photographs of
the soldiers killed in the war. Kerry's mum ran
into the room when she heard screaming. She sat
on the floor sobbing in grief. It was her husband,
she knew it was over.

Kirsty Haines (12)
Dodderhill School, Droitwich Spa

Love Can Die

They were both young and vulnerable. Young love at first sight some say but underneath it was unreal; they hadn't realised yet. It was too late to realise. They married, had children and settled down.
Only thirty years later when they were alone did they realise love *can* die …

Anna Blaney (12)
Dodderhill School, Droitwich Spa

Day In The Life Of A Child

Waking up this morning it didn't feel the same.
Was I somebody completely different? I felt like
myself. I didn't want to go to school today only
because of dreaded French. None of the other
lessons were as bad. I didn't want to go but
suddenly life changed rapidly …

Georgina Downes (12)
Dodderhill School, Droitwich Spa

A Night To Remember

The night of the hunt ball arrived, she had longed
to go to see Sam. When she stepped out of the
car, Sam came past, stopped and admired her.
She took his arm and they walked in together. All
night they stayed together, danced and talked.
They fell in love!

Jessica Skuse (12)
Dodderhill School, Droitwich Spa

137

Below The Lake

Below the castle lake, deep down, came muffled screams. If only he had been faster, this wouldn't have happened. Brian stood at the edge of the lake, gripping the rope that would've saved the hostages. Brian threw his gaming gloves at the computer, he couldn't be worse at this game!

Abigail Morris (13)

Dodderhill School, Droitwich Spa

Remember

Evening draws near, the strong familiar smell of smoke rises. My little moth friends came out to play. The sun disappearing behind a black velvet curtain. *Bang, fizz!* I carefully dodge the clouds of smoke. Who's invading? Bombs, guns? Nothing dangerous of the sort. Remember, remember the fifth of November.

Philippa Jacob (12)
Dodderhill School, Droitwich Spa

Shadows Of The Night

We were walking. The sky was dark and the path
was cold. We were alone. The only sounds were
the cars in the distance and the leaves swaying in
the trees. There were shadows, shadows lurking
in the darkness. They were moving in the night.
There were eyes always watching.

Nicole Snipe (12)
Dodderhill School, Droitwich Spa

The Monster

The door rattled. It was the monster. The smell of unwashed hair crept under the door. Drums played as it ran. A streak of green as it crept around the corner, she hid under the table. The crocodile's sidekick flew into the room. 'Found you!' shouted Natasha's little brother, Jake.

Annabelle Newland (12)

Dodderhill School, Droitwich Spa

141

The Rescue

He arrived at the house, trying to get in. He saw strange features, heard a howl and a whisper. A dog came running. Next they were in! Looking around they peeked through every room and found the hostages in the living room. They rescued them and ran towards the exit.

Georgina Gibbs (12)

Dodderhill School, Droitwich Spa

A Love-Hate Situation

She turned around saw a tall man. He was the most handsome man she had ever seen. Blond hair, blue eyes. Their eyes met. She smiled, he smiled, it was love at first sight. He walked over to her. He looked her up and down, then walked away. Oh gosh.

Lucy Street (12)
Dodderhill School, Droitwich Spa

143

The Dream That Never Came True

He stood there watching me silently, his eyes as green as emeralds, his lips as red as a rose, his skin gleaming in the sunlight, his hair as soft as a pillow. The girl ran over and clutched his hand and left. My heart sank in deep warm sorrow.

Tasmin Sanghera (12)
Dodderhill School, Droitwich Spa

The Childhood Adventures Of Indiana Jones

Indiana Jones woke ready to face a new adventure. He went into the bathroom and after five minutes of brushing, combing and washing he was ready. He headed straight to the door. He wondered, *how do I get out? Mmm, tricky one.* 'Don't forget your lunch box Indie,' called Mum.

Chloe Derricutt (12)

Dodderhill School, Droitwich Spa

145

I Did Love Him

His golden locks were blowing in the wind as he
slowly walked towards me. His twinkling blue
eyes were staring deeply into mine. When he
smiled his pearly teeth glowed in the sunlight. I
did love him.
'Cut, that's a wrap.' And he turned around and
walked towards his wife.

Natasha Ratti (13)
Dodderhill School, Droitwich Spa

The Dark Rider

As black as night, it speeds through the wood.
Narrowly avoiding trees, it crashes through
fences and gates. It is a demon. Its name suits it.
Then the teacher shouts, 'Hold on! You're going
far too fast! Stop that horse!'
That was when I fell off the great black stallion.

Luze Cavelle-Lock (12)
Dodderhill School, Droitwich Spa

Daydream Nightmare

Jessica entered the empty, creepy room belonging to Mrs Vivit. Jessica thought it was the end of her life, as she knew the evil blood-curdling creature always carried a deadly weapon and she knew it used it. But luckily for her, Jessica was only daydreaming again.

Charlotte Arnold (12)
Dodderhill School, Droitwich Spa

Being Bullied

At a supermarket till I peered around. There was a very old school friend of mine; he'd bullied me like no person had ever bullied another, leaving me with bruises and scars. I could feel every punch and kick.

'Are you alright Sir, twenty pounds please!' the shopkeeper asked.

Phoebe Groves (12)

Dodderhill School, Droitwich Spa

149

The Prowler

Prowling around the den the creature takes a sniff of the air; the scent is fresh and so is the trap. Pacing, pacing. He takes a step out onto unknown territory. He darts here and there, scrambles up the tablecloth towards the prey. The mouse picks up the cheese.

Jessica Appleton (12)
Dodderhill School, Droitwich Spa

The New Car

Whizzing down the road in my jet-black sports
car I felt on top of the world. Roof down, hair
whipping in my face but, just then, I saw a car
coming straight at me. Then, nothing.
'Thank you for riding on the virtual simulator,
please exit to your left.'

Charlotte Bourne (13)
Dodderhill School, Droitwich Spa

The Cat

I stared at the beautiful cat, silky black, but still in the grass, eyes closed. Lifeless, a feline majesty, once strong and graceful, now inert. Suddenly the cat's eyes opened: topaz-blue she gazed in relief, she stretched, moving off - feline prowess at its best after a well-earned nap.

Sophie Condlyffe (13)
Dodderhill School, Droitwich Spa

The Tree

I heard the leaves rustling on the tree, then I heard a loud *bang*. I looked out the window; the old oak tree had gone. Then I remembered they had to cut it down. If they'd left it, the tree would fall on my house.

Ellie Morriss (12)

Dodderhill School, Droitwich Spa

Falling!

I was falling through the air, clouds swooping by. I began to turn and spin, feeling awfully sick. Both of my ears popped, I couldn't hear anything. Then a light came on above my head, 'Please fasten your seatbelts'.

Jennifer Cahill (12)
Dodderhill School, Droitwich Spa

As They Swim

Blue waters waving by, high to low. They are
friendly, they might say hi or just give a goodbye.
They come round here and there. Oh look at
all my friendly friends. They're cute and sweet,
lovely dolphins.

Anna Dowty (11)
Dodderhill School, Droitwich Spa

155

Under The Sea

Diving into the glimmering aqua sea, exploring
vast amounts of tropical fish, crumbling coral
beneath. Venturing further than I should go,
depressingly all breath disappeared, cold crept
in. Floating up, wondering where Mum was,
waves crunched over me, water gushing inside.
Watching the world disappearing through the
array of blue.

Sophie Baker (13)

Dodderhill School, Droitwich Spa

A Love Story

Glistening black hair waving in the wind, eyes browner then a bar of chocolate, standing tall and proud, showing he is in charge. I have always loved that about him. Whilst staring, I feel a tug at my leg.

'Can we go see the lions now? The gorillas are boring.'

Emilia Meredith (12)
Dodderhill School, Droitwich Spa

I Love Him

I love him so much I could not love anything as much as him. He is the best in the world. He is always there for me if I need him. I could not live without him. Best thing is we go for walks together, my dog and me.

Victoria Weaver (13)

Dodderhill School, Droitwich Spa

The Dangerous Wood

Skipping across the field of daisies, unaware of her surroundings, so frightened, as the eyes appeared from the trees and the path folded up behind her. Gaily she rushed to Grandma's, fruit spilling from her basket. Little Red Riding Hood fell to the ground, tumbling. She was now no more.

Emily Brazier (14)
Dodderhill School, Droitwich Spa

159

The Interview

That was his last interview for the day. He had
done well. The job was almost guaranteed. While
the pay and position were good, there was some
discomfort. He didn't think that he was reporting
to a person who could lift him to the next level.
He silently walked away.

Shahbaz Hassan (13)

Hijaz College, Nuneaton

The Infamous

There he stood, with injuries beyond compare
and didn't falter one second. The large figure
that was standing on top of him vanished. His
companion was looking healthier already. Not
knowing that this man took all of his injuries for
him. The hero stood firm then collapsed with a
smile.

Amir Shehu (15)

Hijaz College, Nuneaton

Playground

It was a jungle. I stared, my jaw slack. The queen lazily surveyed her pride, her golden hair shining in sunlight. Her cat eyes fixed upon me. She mentally judged me. A smirk curled her lip, but I stood defiant. She grinned.

My mother whispered, 'Have a good first day!'

Kirtey Verma (15)
Holy Trinity School, Kidderminster

That Fateful Day

I stood in awe, looking at the tremendous glory of the supreme structure that was built to perfection, with every detail accounted for. My eyes were transfixed by its beauty, transported to a better place. And then my mother dragged me from the window where that chocolate cake lay.

Rachael King (15)
Holy Trinity School, Kidderminster

The Thief Of Hearts

Once upon a time the Queen of Hearts made some lovely jammy tarts. But, as she was putting a new batch of jammy apricot tarts in the oven, the Knave of Hearts stole the lovely jammy tarts and he wolfed them down. Oh what a boring jam tart was he!

Ciara Holmes (11)

John Kyrle High School Sixth Form College, Ross-on-Wye

Hunting The Dead

Pipes burst spraying water, sparks of light shot out of electrical wires. Spiderwebs hung in my face, itching and irritating my skin. In the distance I could make out a small figure crouched on its knees, grossly ripping off shreds of skin and meat off an unfortunate lifeless creature.

Tasha Hughes (12)

John Kyrle High School Sixth Form College, Ross-on-Wye

165

Surprise

Everyone rushing madly around. People putting up decorations and blowing up balloons. Plates full of food being placed on tables. Will they be ready in time? Will it be a success? Off go the lights. 'Ssh!' Everyone is quiet. Footsteps can be heard. Poppers go off … 'Surprise! Happy birthday!'

Abbey Colwell (11)

John Kyrle High School Sixth Form College, Ross-on-Wye

Scared

She tiptoed into the mansion. Her steps echoed loudly. It was all black then suddenly a bright beam shot out and ghastly sounds emerged. She wanted to run but was immediately stopped by a strong force. Her heart was racing she couldn't describe what she saw - or what she felt!

Nikita Bagga (11)

John Kyrle High School Sixth Form College, Ross-on-Wye

The Follower

It was right behind me. Every step I took it was getting closer and closer. I looked back but all I could see was the murky mist around me. I was running as fast as the wind. My heart was pounding.
Then I woke up … it was just a dream.

Freya Jarrett (11)
John Kyrle High School Sixth Form College, Ross-on-Wye

Trapped

The bird, closed off, trapped in mankind's metal prison, once so happy, so free until the hands of human clasped it. Cold and alone the bird can no longer spread its elegant wing. Its colour snatched from its world, just a black and white film; death the only way out.

Olivia Mace (11)

John Kyrle High School Sixth Form College, Ross-on-Wye

169

Goldilocks - The Court Case!

'Order in the court today! On trial is Goldilocks for a number of crimes, including theft, breaking and entering. Goldilocks, the crimes you have committed are: breaking and entering, theft and damage to property. How do you plead?'

'Not guilty!'

'And what do the jury think?'

'She is guilty.'

'Huh!'

Rebecca Collins (11)

John Kyrle High School Sixth Form College, Ross-on-Wye

Disappeared!

Once there was an old man who lived on his own. One day he decided to go on a walk up a mountain. At the top he found a cave so he went inside and there was a sort of glowing figure in there. Then there was a scream and …

Lewis Fletcher (12)

John Kyrle High School Sixth Form College, Ross-on-Wye

When The Pixies Flew

The pixies flew around and around, darting from side to side, dodging leaves and flowers, one knocking off pretty, pink flower petals on the way. Spinning and swirling like a ballerina prancing to the melody. Their light as golden as syrup was shining bright in the gloomy dead of night …

Lucy Dean (11)

John Kyrle High School Sixth Form College, Ross-on-Wye

The Town Of Cobra

It was a cold dark night in the town of Cobra.
The alley was pitch-black, nothing could be seen.
It also smelt like the sewers from Ross-on-Wye.
The brave and fearless kids: Timmy, Katie and
Samantha walked down the alley … never to be
seen again.

Hannah Hayes (12)
John Kyrle High School Sixth Form College, Ross-on-Wye

The Woods

It was a dark foggy night as Bobby walked through the woods. The branches poked him like arthritic fingers through the shadows of darkness, flying through the air like a cape upon a rider. He heard footsteps. He ran then slipped on the boggy path … he awoke to see Mum.

Emily Mince (11)
John Kyrle High School Sixth Form College, Ross-on-Wye

Mr Green

It was a short cut I didn't want to take. Mr Green
shot squirrels and ate children but I couldn't be
late for Mum. My heart was hammering as I crept
round the corner of his bungalow. Peering round
the corner there he was lying in a pool of
blood …

Aimee Stevenson (11)

John Kyrle High School Sixth Form College, Ross-on-Wye

Night Fright!

As I walked down the eerie and creepy staircase,
the candyfloss cobwebs brushed against my bright
fluorescent clothes. As I crept step by step, I
heard a creaking sound. I stopped and turned
around. As I turned around a breeze of wind blew
in front of my face. I paused …

Clare Bailey (12)

John Kyrle High School Sixth Form College, Ross-on-Wye

The Mysterious Jog

It was a dark gloomy morning. As I finished tying my laces, I felt the cold soft breeze on the back of my neck. As I was darting in and out of the puddles I felt my clothes tighten and a mysterious face pull me back. Should I turn around?

Luke Craig (11)
John Kyrle High School Sixth Form College, Ross-on-Wye

Scary Surprise

I ran through the woods, ducking under every branch. It was dark now; the only light was the twinkling of the stars. I could hear leaves crunching under my feet, trees blowing in the wind. I ran faster.
Finally I reached the cottage.
'Happy birthday Lauren!' My friends cheered.

Lauren Darkes (11)
John Kyrle High School Sixth Form College, Ross-on-Wye

That Special Moment!

The friends got out of the car. The echo of them
complimenting his house filled Jim's proud ears.
'Beautiful, wonderful, out of this world!'
They then walked past the house, took a path
around the side of the building. A rotting shack
came into view. Sadly, his home!

Fred Hunt (11)

John Kyrle High School Sixth Form College, Ross-on-Wye

The Thing In The Woods

I was nearly at the end of the path, dark trees
creeping over me, scary noises coming from
every direction and glowing creepy eyes. I carried
on walking, I kept looking over my shoulder. I was
still walking and was still looking. I looked over
my shoulder and then …

Tanith Green (12)

John Kyrle High School Sixth Form College, Ross-on-Wye

The Fat Black Cat

There was a big fat black cat that loved jumping
on walls, but his owner wouldn't let him out very
much, so that's why he is so fat. All he could do
was laze around so eating was just something to
do with his life - every day and all day.

Kim Holder (11)

John Kyrle High School Sixth Form College, Ross-on-Wye

The Deathly Silence

Creak! Sniffle, sniffle.
I whispered, 'Hello, is anybody there?' I jumped,
not expecting a reply but there was a reply.
'Yes, there is someone or shall I say something!'
The reply seemed to shudder through the
walls and through me. The people in Pompeii
screamed.

Jack Lindley (11)
John Kyrle High School Sixth Form College, Ross-on-Wye

The Shadows!

I lay trembling in my bed. A scary figure emerged
on my creaky floorboards, from the leaves of
the trees outside. I hid, terrified of the petrifying
sounds. I saw shimmers of light.
Then … Dad came in and said, 'Alright, we've just
had a power cut.'
'Phew, thank God!'

Emily Reynolds (11)
John Kyrle High School Sixth Form College, Ross-on-Wye

183

Surrounded

The screeches and cries I hear through the greasy mist, footsteps sinking into the thick slimy mud, shadows seeming to get closer and closer. The sun is fading away as the clouds cover it up. Then suddenly *splat!* My face hits the dirt. I jump up to see a ... fly?

Joseph Fear (11)
John Kyrle High School Sixth Form College, Ross-on-Wye

Trick Or Treat

I went out trick or treating. I went to a house that looked scary and saw a person standing very still. I said, 'This looks scary.' I knocked on the door, no answer. Then suddenly I heard a noise. I screamed and ran all the way home.

Rebecca Gardner (12)

John Kyrle High School Sixth Form College, Ross-on-Wye

Untitled

A girl was running fast in a race, trying to win for her county. At that moment in time she just fainted, couldn't catch her breath. She had to get up and keep running. So her mate behind picked her up. In the end she won her trophy.

Casey Abbott (12)

Moorside High School, Werrington

Untitled

A man was driving his new car on the M1 and just as he turned off junction 24 a lorry smashed straight in the back of him and sent him flying into a bush. The lorry driver called an ambulance, they looked in the car and he was … gone!

Jordan Walker (13)
Moorside High School, Werrington

187

The Haunted House

I walked into the scary house. I could hear things scratching around, but then I heard a big *bang!* I went to look what it was. It was a big fat hairy monster. It was really scary, then he chased me. I never went back.

Thomas Hunt (12)
Moorside High School, Werrington

The Slippery Night

It was a cold frosty night. Chloe and Beth were
trudging around the park, suddenly someone
jumped out in front of them. Beth slipped and
badly hurt her ankle Chloe took her to the
hospital, her ankle was broken!
After a few hours she was able to go home.

Katie Meredith (12)

Moorside High School, Werrington

The Haunted House

I was on my way back from school when I saw a dark deserted house. I saw three girls go in and I watched for five minutes but they never came out. I heard screams and saw shadows.
That night on the news, it said three girls were missing …

Emma Grainger (12)
Moorside High School, Werrington

Humpty Dumpty's Disaster

Humpty Dumpty an egg head was he, he sat on
a wall and was full of glee. But poor old Humpty,
because he was round, slipped off the wall and fell
to the ground. Now Humpty has a new home, in
Mr Fox's belly, poor thing!

Beth Clews (11)

Moorside High School, Werrington

191

The Shadow

The girl stepped into her gloomy room. She heard a noise and turned around and saw a shadow in the distance, then there was a loud *bang* and the lights turned on. To her amazement she saw her sister in the same place where the shadow had been!

Louise Weston (11)

Moorside High School, Werrington

The Pig And The Barn

One day there was a fat pig who ate and ate, he couldn't stop. All the other animals had a meeting to help him and agreed on stealing his food. When the fat pig came to eat there was no food left so he started to eat the barn!

Jordan Wheeler (11)

Moorside High School, Werrington

The Chaser

I was walking down the street. I walked around the corner then I saw a shadow of a giant thing. I went to look, there was a monster. It looked at me and started coming towards me! I ran to my house, it got into my house then suddenly disappeared ...

Alex Lovatt (11)
Moorside High School, Werrington

Sewer Savage

Its shadow scurried the pipes, its stenches reeked
throughout. Emily craned her neck; in attempt
to spot the vile creature. Then she felt it, a snap
at her leg - oh, the pain. She kicked and shook
however it didn't release. So Emily gave up,
condemning herself to the unknown savage ...

Farrah Barber (12)
Moorside High School, Werrington

Little Red Punk

Once there was a girl called Little Red Punk. She had bright red hair and a black coat. To have fun she used to get in a fight with the big wolf. She always won.

One day her grandma challenged her to a fight. Punk lost, with a flat nose!

Sam Milward (11)

Moorside High School, Werrington

Sleeping Beauty

The prince leapt through the forest of thorns.
He tore down the sharp vines with a twist of his
hand.
'I'm coming for you my … argh!' *Bump!* 'Mummy!
I have a boo-boo.'
He found the princess, kissed her and … 'Five
more minutes,' he said, turning over.

Chloe Warren (11)

Moorside High School, Werrington

197

Trench Boy

Bang! Crash! Boom! Bullets were firing past my head. Dead bodies covered the trench with entry and exit wounds. The snow was deep, coloured red where the blood had soaked. Then, without warning, *kaboom!* A giant plane covered all exits. The only way out was over the trench bank …

Ryan Fox (12)
Moorside High School, Werrington

Escape

There was a young boy who was chased by a three-headed dog. He ran into a dark forest, which was haunted by a poltergeist. Then he saw a magic coin, he rubbed it and then he went into a fairytale where Sleeping Beauty was, but the poltergeist appeared ...

James Brindley (12)
Moorside High School, Werrington

199

Untitled

There was a boy called Jake, he liked to play on his Xbox, he never came off it.
Then one day a storm came and Jake had to play 'Storm Saber 5' to clear the storm. When he'd finished his mum came home and brought Jake 'COD 6'.

Daniel Lowe (12)
Moorside High School, Werrington

Taken

'Boo!' The ghost jumped out from the wardrobe.
'Argh!' Me and my best friends stood silent,
shocked. The woman with a sock on her head
stood and took Amy, then went back in the
wardrobe. Since then we couldn't remember
what happened and didn't see Amy again, until
now …

Dana Carter (13)
Moorside High School, Werrington

201

Men In Black: Springfield Version

'Boom!' The alien ship crashed down in Springfield. As everyone gathered round Homer and Bart were running to it with massive guns and shot the ship into orbit. Then Bart got out the memory laser 2000 and zapped everyone in Springfield. Homer and Bart were the Men In Black!

Edward Scragg (11)

Moorside High School, Werrington

The Moonlit Hill

As I walked up the moonlit hill I saw a terrifying
shadow. I looked up and there it was, a werewolf.
It stood broad on its strong hind legs, its eyes
were as red as the evening sun, its claws were as
sharp as daggers. Then it saw me …

Ben Smith (12)
Moorside High School, Werrington

Untitled

As Cinderella left the ball her glass slipper fell off
and was found by Prince Charming.
The next day Prince Charming turned up at the
door of Cinderella's house and forced Cinderella
to wear the slipper. It didn't fit because she had
grown overnight. Unlucky chucky!

Brandon Unwin (12)

Moorside High School, Werrington

The Antelope And The Squirrel

Philip the antelope was walking through the forest
when he got his antler caught in a tree.
'Oh no,' he cried, 'somebody help!'
Suddenly a squirrel appeared. 'I'll help you,' he
said. He untangled the antlers. They remained
best friends forever and always ate nuts together.

Chloe Brown (12)
Moorside High School, Werrington

Football Mania

Ashley, Arthur and Kane were interested in football. They took turns to take their footballs into school.

One day, Arthur took in a brand new Nike football. It was expensive. While playing, the year 11s kicked Arthur's football, kicked it into the roof. It rolled down and they caught it!

Samuel Bateman (13)

Moorside High School, Werrington

The Monkey And The Squirrel

Once there was a monkey who lived in a tree,
his friend was a squirrel and they both cherished
mangos.
One day there was a loud crash; they hopped on
a boat with their mangos and sailed to Hawaii.
There they lived in a new tree and started
collecting coconuts.

Ellen Thorpe (12)
Moorside High School, Werrington

Monster Beneath

A shiver ran up my spine, as a bony hand shadowed over the pavement. Making my way through the graveyard I stopped and stared as an object moved past my eye at speed. Running, the fog drifted past and squinting I made out a solid object running towards me.

Annie Harvey (12)
Moorside High School, Werrington

Mile Per Hour

I got on my quad and zoomed into a field. I pulled a wheelie at 40mph and braked, sending the front two wheels pounding to the ground. I got to a corner at 80mph and just about made it and then just made it to a full stop.

Jordan Botham (12)
Moorside High School, Werrington

Ghost House

There was a house placed by a graveyard where ghosts roamed the land. Three girls had been dared to go in the house to stay the night. They walked through the house and placed their bags down and went up the stairs … they were never seen again.

Amy Bullock (12)
Moorside High School, Werrington

Hall Spooks!

'Lucy, what's this?' said Mum.
'It's a letter about the trip to Hall Spooks.'
'I will send it into school so that you can go.'
She walked into Hall Spooks, the door opened on
its own; a hand rested on her shoulder … there
was nobody there! What was it?

Hannah Whitehall (12)
Moorside High School, Werrington

Darkness

The trees swayed in the dark gloomy night, a mysterious howl came out of nowhere. The leaves on the floor which had fallen off the trees, twisted and turned in the wind. Something horrifically tall towered over me and roared, leaving me with just one leg to stand on.

Leah Nelson (13)

Moorside High School, Werrington

It Does What It Says On The Tin

Lee Bourne has big curly hair. He goes to the shop and buys shampoo called 'Wash and Go'. He goes home to wash his hair. The shampoo gets rid of his hair! He tries to sue the shop. The court says no, it does what it says on the tin!

Nick Bourne (12)

Moorside High School, Werrington

The Worst First Day At High School

I bought a slush drink on my first day and walked down the corridor with it. A boy was running, he ran straight into me and my slush went all over me! It was only break-time so I had to sit in cold sticky chocolate slush all day!

Shalon Laidler (12)
Moorside High School, Werrington

The Wolf In The Woods

There was once a girl riding in a wood on her BMX, her name was Leah. She rode to a tree so she could eat, when suddenly a wolf jumped out. She thought and gave it her MP3 player. It let her pass. She then got home to her mates.

Tom Price (12)

Moorside High School, Werrington

Fashion Show Disaster

Cheryl had a dilemma. She wanted to perform
in the fashion show but, when she was getting
dressed, she caught her heel in her dress and
it tore a big hole in the back. She was upset.
Cheryl's best friend didn't turn up so she decided
to use her dress.

Beth Trivett (12)

Moorside High School, Werrington

The Spooky Sleep

Suddenly a loud creak boomed across the floorboards. It was only me there. I walked downstairs to find that the door was open, leading out into the night sky. It sent shivers down my spine, something came into the house. I woke up and found it was all a dream.

Callum Edge (12)
Moorside High School, Werrington

Secrets!

In a small village lived little Adam, he didn't have many friends so he was pleased when Penelope moved in next door. He took a certain liking to her and they soon got to be best friends but Penelope had secrets, secrets nobody would ever find out, or would they?

Laura Cash (12)

Moorside High School, Werrington

In The Darkness

I wasn't alone. The mysterious shape was coming towards me. The eerie shadow moved gracefully in the moonlight as it raced after me. I turned around and ran for my life. I only had one question for myself - was I going to make it out alive?

Rebecca Littlehales (13)
Moorside High School, Werrington

A Skeletal Fate

I was running, running from something that I didn't quite understand. Running from a creature that was monstrous. I was running from something that was after me … What was it after, something that I'd got or just me? Suddenly a skeletal hand dragged me back into complete darkness …

April Whitehurst (12)
Moorside High School, Werrington

My Last Day

It rained almost all night. My feet were soggy and I'd given up on trying to stay dry. The jungle seemed to look down on me. There was no footpath to follow anymore, I was just lost! I stared up at the sky, I knew this was my last day …

Lucy Goodstadt (12)

Moorside High School, Werrington

221

Lifted Like A Feather

As swallows fly higher and higher, this feeling within me is carried afar. Arms spread out wide, feeling the skies. I start to wonder, long for this feeling to make me rise, fly like those birds. Then a jolt of air that comes from nowhere lifts me to the heavens.

Emma Tulley (12)
Moorside High School, Werrington

The Hunter Becomes The Hunted

My bare feet pounded the forest floor as ravenous wolves snapped at my heels. I ran, but wasn't fast enough as a white she-wolf sank her razor-sharp canines into my ankle. I screamed, tumbled to the ground and the she-wolf delivered a fatal bite to my throat.

Kiera Fawcett (12)

Moorside High School, Werrington

Untitled

It was a Halloween night. Three girls called Emma, Issy, Bella went to Alton Towers Scare Fest. As they were walking through the haunted house, Bella disappeared!
Emma said, 'Where's Bella?'
Issy said, 'Don't' know.' So they carried on walking. But then Issy disappeared! Emma never saw them again.

Madeleine James (12)
Moorside High School, Werrington

Skittle Red Riding Hood

Little Red Riding Hood was skipping through the forest. Meanwhile the big bad wolf, tired of being chased by the woodcutter, was lying in wait. As Red Riding Hood skipped past the big bad wolf bowled a rock at her, this flattened her. He then ate her delicious cakes!

Jordan Lander (12)

Moorside High School, Werrington

The Man Who Had No Sense!

There was a man who had no sense. He climbed a glass wall to see what was on the other side! He was flying a helicopter and was cold, so turned off the fan! Once he scared himself, he thought he saw a monster but it was his own reflection!

Robert Mapperson (11)
Moorside High School, Werrington

The Object

Everyone looked up into the sky. There seemed to be a massive unidentified flying object just hovering there, no movement was made. Throughout the years there still had been no movement, nothing had come out of it, and nothing had gone in. Then something had happened, the UFO suddenly opened …

Lucy Tomkinson (12)

Moorside High School, Werrington

Missed Lunch

The fox could see in the distance, his target, a small white rabbit. It started to run. Faster and faster it went, and then … pounce! The fox looked down. He had missed his dinner. The fox then walked away downheartedly as the rabbit sniggered, hidden behind a bush far away.

Emily Woolley (12)
Moorside High School, Werrington

Mr Lemon And The House

There once lived a Mr lemon. One day he went into a haunted house thinking that it was a ride! Then he heard screams so he started walking faster and faster into darkness. Then suddenly something attacked him and he wasn't seen again.

Lewis Adams (12)

Moorside High School, Werrington

White Snow

Mother on the frozen window seat sewing, voice smoking as blood falls to chiffon. It ran in the family - soon her daughter couldn't breathe, lying in frost, unmoving, recently brushed hair a crown. Stepmother stayed inside for the warmth. And then *he* came, and she couldn't speak anything but apples.

Rebecca Wheeler (17)
Pershore High School, Pershore

Cinderella

The princess had achieved happiness. Ugly sisters disposed of, large inheritance fund, the prince nearly in her grasp. She stared into his eyes with intent, he only had one thing left to say before fate was sealed. He leant in close, her breath on his face, 'I'm sorry, I'm gay.'

Alex Woodman (17)

Pershore High School, Pershore

The Clue's In The Murder

My heart thudded like a bass drum. I took
steadying breaths as adrenalin pulsated through
me. My blood was liquid tension. I knew the
murderer and I had to tell someone. Six steps
forward and I darted through the door.
'It was Colonel Mustard with the candlestick in
the ballroom.'

Elisabeth Graham (17)
Pershore High School, Pershore

Red Riding Hood

Walking through the wood with basket in hand,
coat buttoned to the top, Red Riding Hood
had an epiphany. Big teeth, big eyes and big
ears, Grandma appeared to have in this flash
forward. Maybe she'd wait another day to go to
Grandma's, just to be on the safe side.

Katherine Green (17)
Pershore High School, Pershore

233

Alice In Wonderland

Skipping through the daisy field, she fell down a rabbit hole after catching a glimpse of a curious rabbit tapping a pocket watch. Alice fell down into a magical world of grinning cats, croquet queens, mad hatters who had tea parties, shrinking sweets. But who believed Alice after she returned?

Melissa Creese (17)
Pershore High School, Pershore

The Prince And The Dragon

In a land of mystical creatures and terror, a young prince by the name of Lyca, wished to find a wife, proud and noble. A great danger filled their world, as a dragon had captured a young maiden girl. The brave prince saved the young maiden, finding his true love.

Holly-Elizabeth Toney (13)
Pershore High School, Pershore

'Til Death Do Us Part

Sarah stood in the doorway, torn. He was there
- close enough to touch; but he was with another
and they had been married. As her beloved kissed
his new wife; Sarah closed her eyes, took a deep
breath and returned, unseen, to her grave - for he
was hers no longer.

Sophie Harbridge (13)
Pershore High School, Pershore

The Goal!

The match was close; in defence opportunities to score were limited. With the goalkeeper down and the opposition running menacingly towards him, the ball came in and he headed it hard. After hitting the post it crossed the line. The fans cheered loudly ...for the opposition - his first own goal.

Ryan Cooper (13)
Pershore High School, Pershore

237

Unstill Waters

Ten men, one boat. The 'Pursuer' and its crew were on a cargo run to India, but beneath, a storm was brewing. The waves crashed against the ship. The Kraken rose, thunder roared as it picked them off to a watery grave. And then the waters remained still, but waiting …

Michael Wheatley (13)

Pershore High School, Pershore

The Cat And The Fiddle

Hey diddle diddle the cat who played fiddle said
to the cow who looked down, 'Go find the man
on the moon.'
So the cow jumped and the dog laughed. After
the cow jumped over the moon the dish ran away
with the spoon, as they were a perfect pair!

Emily Bitcon (14)
Pershore High School, Pershore

239

A Day In The Life Of A Princess

She woke up, changed and ordered her tea while her maid brushed her gorgeous hair. The passing of the crown was today. She was so scared she thought she was going to muck it up. In the ceremony she got everything perfect and went to bed happy … and a queen.

Rosie Bond (13)

Pershore High School, Pershore

Wasteland

The mother cheetah clambered down from her tree, her young followed hungry and weak. She prowled around the wasteland for her prey. At 45mph this brute force is unstoppable. In this abandoned wasteland you can't hide, its sharp teeth around the throat of the poor zebra. Blood everywhere, silence returns.

Ryan Branfield (14)
Pershore High School, Pershore

The Dangers Of Myth Telling

Sitting, gazing at the fire, listening to my favourite myth of the unknown beast. After listening to it many times I still find myself on the edge of my seat. The best bit is next. The monster kills … when suddenly my father is snatched into the darkness. No sound remains.

Jared White (13)

Pershore High School, Pershore

The Earthquake

The family was washing-up. Suddenly, the ground trembled, again and again. Trembling, the little family were getting scared. They huddled up in the corner of the room, waiting for it to stop. But it didn't. It got louder and louder until …
'Dad!' cried Susie. 'The doll's house door's stuck.'

Lauren Osborne (13)
Pershore High School, Pershore

The Girl With A Secret Life: Hannah Montana

In the day she's a normal girl who lives an ordinary life, at night she's a teen pop-star she's known at school as Miley Stewart but around the world she's known as Hannah Montana. Her secret is safe with her family so she can live the best of both worlds.

Katie Dawson (13)

Pershore High School, Pershore

Untitled

Our hands entwined together. I could feel his body next to mine. My breath quickened and we started to move. Sweat dripped down my back, the feeling was intense. I closed my eyes and let out a scream. We stopped; I sighed with relief and stepped off the roller coaster.

Rebecca Dawkes (17)
Pershore High School, Pershore

The Chase

I saw a bull on a moor. It stared at me. I ran, the bull ran after me. Faster, faster, help! Help! It was catching me. Where could I hide? Where could I run to? How could I escape from this wild animal? 'Wake up Kieran, time to get up.'

Kieran Rifat (12)

River House School, Henley in Arden

The Scary Night

It was late one night when I got into bed and I felt something moving at my feet. I leapt up and checked the bottom of my bed. I thought my hamster had escaped again. I pulled back the covers! Prepared to smile but, oh no, a boa constrictor … !

Scott Humphries (11)
River House School, Henley in Arden

Dinnertime

Tom stared in horror when he stood in front of
an eight-foot monster, with blood dripping from
his mouth. The monster walked towards Tom and
pulled out a sharp blade and tried to slice Tom in
the stomach.
'Come on Tom, dinner's ready. Put your book
down!'

Ryan Laverty (14)
River House School, Henley in Arden

The Storm

It was dark, damp and raining a thunderstorm.
The children heard a big *bang* and a creaky door.
They started to scream but then it started to rain
harder and louder. They started to hear ghost
noises but then they found out it was a tape
recorder!

Lewis Coulton (14)

River House School, Henley in Arden

My Telepathic Friend

My friend is weird, he has a telepathic mind, he can pick up stuff with his mind.
One day he ripped our teacher in half with his mind … then I wasn't friends with him anymore.
He is a freak. Who knows, he might come for me …

Brandon Curzon-Hope (12)
River House School, Henley in Arden

My Doll's House

The towering walls crumbled around me bit by bit. Every piece of the house was falling into smithereens. The furniture fell into a broken heap like a bonfire. The snapped bookcase lay forgotten in a corner, surrounded by its scattered books. That was the end of my modern doll's house.

Lydia Stansbury (12)
St Mary's RC High School, Hereford

251

The Instrument Of Torture

I stared at it, hatred burning intensely in my
loathing, emerald eyes. Its countless spikes
sinister, narrow, sadistic; a replica instrument of
medieval torture. You can't fathom how much
I strongly detested that thing. I slowly lifted
the heavily rusted, ancient watering can to the
terracotta pot of the cactus …

Catherine Beaumont (12)
St Mary's RC High School, Hereford

Death Day

I was walking down the corridor then bumped
into a stranger, we chatted and I invited him
round. I laid out refreshments; there was a knock
at the door. I opened it and greeted him. He took
off his coat and grinned menacingly. That was the
night I died.

Abigail Powell (11)
St Mary's RC High School, Hereford

Running

I was running, running, as fast as I could. Sweat poured down my face, but I couldn't stop, they were catching up. I was exhausted but I had to carry on. I pushed myself, 'Come on,' I told myself, 'Get ahead.'
I finished the race in five minutes, thirty seconds.

Millie Manning (11)
St Mary's RC High School, Hereford

All Alone As Time Ran Out On Me

She ran and ran. She ran as if her life depended on it. She passed the empty streets, all alone in the darkness she ran. Her golden watch ticked. *Tick, tick, tick, tick*. She stopped; it was all over … the shop was closed.

Rosalie Herrera-Henshaw (11)
St Mary's RC High School, Hereford

Galloping

She kicked her horse forward, he was nervous.
They started to gallop. She could hardly stay on.
She reached for the reins, her hands fumbled
and she slipped and screamed, 'Help me! I can't
control my horse!'
She closed her eyes and the merry-go-round
came to a halt.

Kirsty Myers (11)
St Mary's RC High School, Hereford

The Killer

He stumbled about in a desperate plight to escape. The expert weapons of the murderer were poised. With a quick slash it was over, the mangled body lay limp on my lawn. The neighbour's cat, Claws, the killer, had struck again, the bird was dead.
'Oh Claws!' I moaned.

Grace Rider (12)
St Mary's RC High School, Hereford

Ghosts!

I walked silently through the graveyard. I sensed something or someone watching me, slowly I carried on walking. I was getting more worried every step. I saw something moving behind a lonely grave. I edged my way towards it. 'Ooh!' I gasped. 'Ghosts!' Screaming, I ran all the way home.

Alice Eckley (11)
St Mary's RC High School, Hereford

The Eternal Hole

I was the hero fighting the bad. I was after Mr
Invisible. We climbed over the bridge over the
eternal hole. I fell just managing to grasp on to
one of the metal planks. Slipping every second, I
was going to fall … I did!
Then found myself in the playground.

Katie Powell (11)
St Mary's RC High School, Hereford

Running

I ran as fast as I could, tripping on dropped pencils, slipping on the floor. Shaking in fear, I clutched my side in pain, I had to keep running, gasping for breath; I heard a door open ahead of me.

'You're late for maths, Molly, that's a detention after school.'

Rebecca Young (11)
St Mary's RC High School, Hereford

The Stranger

Knock, knock. No! He'd come for me. I was doomed! My breath quickened, growing more urgent. The door handle seemed to be telling me to open it, the door creaked open. He stood there, grinning madly. His rounded glasses shone in the blinding sun.
My little brother had come home.

Danielle Gabb (11)
St Mary's RC High School, Hereford

The Cursed Shoes

I sit in the shop window, bored! Unexpectedly I see these amazing shoes. Do they have them in my size? Yes! I take them home and play football … but I trip and cut my knee and break my ankle! Anyway, stupid shoes, they deserve to be where I put them.

Ross Hutchinson (11)

St Mary's RC High School, Hereford

Dark Happenings

The vampires on my left drew closer. So did the werewolves on my right. The six heads of the dogs in front and behind me snarled, ready to pounce. Light shone over the trees in the forest clearing. 'Twas a signal. Suddenly as one movement, they pounced ...
I woke up.

Kate Barber (11)

St Mary's RC High School, Hereford

Recipe For Disaster

I entered the building, nobody to be seen. I dashed up the rickety stairs. This was my chance. It was locked! I looked around, still nobody to be seen. I pulled on the rusty handle … I was in! I reached under the bed, it was mine! I grabbed the cookbook.

Conor Kearns (12)

St Mary's RC High School, Hereford

Padding Feet

Silence fell. The clock was ticking in the hall.
Everyone was asleep. I lay awake. Then I heard
the slow pad of feet coming up the stairs. My
heart pounded. The padding got louder and
louder. It sprang. Something landed on
my chest …
I woke up and there was Whiskers!

Megan Shaw (11)
St Mary's RC High School, Hereford

Chaotic Dreams

I lay in a large field. Where was I? I was in an unknown land where there was nothing but grass. I was panicking. I was going crazy. Stupid in fact. I was sweating with fear. All I wanted was to go home. I then was falling … onto my pillow.

Owen Rogers (11)

St Mary's RC High School, Hereford

Mystery Mansion

Darkness fell. Sophie stepped inside. The walls
creaked eerily. She jumped at every sound
and shadow. The first room was completely
dilapidated. She swore she heard a voice Sophie
timidly stepped towards the window and a giant
flash of light blasted in the window. It was only
some lost tourists!

Leah Cottrell (12)
St Mary's RC High School, Hereford

267

The Wolf

Through the dark woodland, terrified, Marie
floundered towards the castle. Relentlessly, the
blood-curdling howl echoed behind her. She ran
faster now, thrashing blindly against the brambles.
The trees seemingly unending, then, at last! The
drawbridge. Aaahh - shut! Was she trapped?
Suddenly, 'Cut!' yelled the director, and Marie
collapsed laughing, exhausted.

Eleanor Brazewell (11)
St Mary's RC High School, Hereford

The Rainbow Fade

Over the clouds, down it came, a leprechaun
riding a sparking cane. As it came down it
spread luck, then it was spotted so things went
a-muck. The spell of truth became wrong from
higgywiggly to inajiggly. So the rainbow wobbled
away, the leprechaun fell, dropping an erase
memory spell.

Hassan Shariff (13)
Sir Graham Balfour High School, Stafford

Halloween On Friday 13th

Halloween, Friday 13th. It was the time for trick or treaters. Abi and Tom sat in the dark living room, waiting. Then suddenly, there was a terrifying scratching at the door! Slowly, Abi answered; there was nobody there! Something touched her leg, she looked down … it was her cat!

Emily Roantree (12)
Whitecross High School, Hereford

Death In The Classroom

I watched in horror as I saw Mrs Slicer with a knife on the wall. I heard a scream. A sickening thump as the knife hit the table and something rolled across the floor … I peered through the door, it was only Mrs Slicer slicing a head off a carrot!

Jessica Ruck (12)

Whitecross High School, Hereford

Masked!

John was in his room reading a book. A scratching noise? He opened the door to nobody. Suddenly a masked man appeared in the mirror with a knife! John ran but was stabbed.
John woke up ... a bad dream but then a scratching on the door ... just a dream?

Thomas Davies (11)

Whitecross High School, Hereford

Cheese Kills

The mouse ran as fast as a rocket, following him
was the brown oriental cat, hell-bent on revenge.
The mouse turned the corner better than the
McLaren team put together. The cat followed,
teeth glistening in the light. The mouse was
cornered, the cat pounced …
Jack paused the DVD.

Richard Hancock (11)
Whitecross High School, Hereford

Halloween Death

It was a spooky Friday night and guess what - it
was Halloween. Harry wasn't very well so he
couldn't go trick or treating. He could hear
somebody so he rushed to the door. My God!
Blood, no head and torn clothes.
'Trick or treat?' Harry died of a heart attack.

Harry Bradbury (11)
Whitecross High School, Hereford

Attack Of The Brains

One day in the middle of nowhere, there lived a scientist, a mad scientist. This scientist came up with a invention that could bring people back to life! It worked great until people's bodies died but not their brains. The brains jumped out of the bodies and killed everyone.

Emily Grubb (11)
Whitecross High School, Hereford

I'm Stuck

One day I was in Miss Morris' English class and I couldn't think of anything to write. I was just sitting there, trying to think of something to write. I was thinking of loads of different things but I didn't like any of them so I decided to write this!

Cara Powell (11)
Whitecross High School, Hereford

A Frightful Night In The Woods

It was a dark misty night; a man was walking his dog through the wood when suddenly strange lights appeared in the sky above him. An overpowering beam of light shot down over the man. A scream! All was quiet in the woods, the man and his dog had vanished!

Marley George (11)
Whitecross High School, Hereford

Untitled

I struggled to get out. The waves smashed the
sides of my boat. A whirlpool! I tried to escape
but it was too strong. I saw a piece of wood and
tried to grab it. It kept slipping from my grasp …
He watched the ant go down the plug hole.

Calum Loveridge (11)
Whitecross High School, Hereford

The Hand

My heart was pounding and my hair stood
up. The door creaked and a hunched shadow
appeared. It had something in its hand. I hid
myself, it moved closer and I started to advance
to the opposite door. I reached for the handle.
Then it appeared … it was my grandad.

Oliver Taylor (11)
Whitecross High School, Hereford

The Deadly Storm

A terrible storm approached and lightning shocked a tree where a fire blazed out of control. Buildings were tumbling down, people and animals getting swallowed up in the blink of an eye. Suddenly the ground went from beneath my feet and I was twisted violently around - would I survive this?

Ryan Meyrick (11)
Whitecross High School, Hereford

Mini Marvels Worcestershire & The West Midlands

Information

We hope you have enjoyed reading this book - and that you will continue to enjoy it in the coming years.

If you like reading and writing, drop us a line or give us a call and we'll send you a free information pack. Alternatively visit our website at **www.youngwriters.co.uk**

Write to:

Young Writers Information,
Remus House,
Coltsfoot Drive,
Peterborough,
PE2 9JX

Tel: (01733) 890066
Email: youngwriters@forwardpress.co.uk